AF751751

Paris

TAKES OVER THE WORLD

I dedicate this book to my Dad, for teaching me about retracing my steps to find something, and always looking backwards when going forwards. I also dedicate this book to my daughter Kiara, and her amazing mind.—KM

Scholastic Australia
An imprint of Scholastic Australia Pty Limited
PO Box 579 Gosford NSW 2250
(ABN 11 000 614 577)
www.scholastic.com.au

Part of the Scholastic Group
Sydney · Auckland · New York · Toronto · London · Mexico City
New Delhi · Hong Kong · Buenos Aires · Puerto Rico

Published by Scholastic Australia in 2022.

Cover design by Hannah Janzen.
Internal design by Nicolette Treanor.

NATIONAL LIBRARY OF AUSTRALIA

A catalogue record for this book is available from the National Library of Australia

ISBN: 978-1-74383-742-9

Typeset in Mrs Ant, Helsing, Harman Script, Harman Deco, Canvas Surly Sans and Carrotflower.

Printed in China by Hang Tai Printing Company Limited.

Scholastic Australia's policy, in association with Hang Tai, is to use papers that are renewable and made efficiently from wood grown in responsibly managed forests, so as to minimise its environmental footprint.

10 9 8 7 6 5 4 3 22 23 24 25 26 / 2

Paris

TAKES OVER THE WORLD

BY KYLA MAY
WITH ZANNI LOUISE

A Scholastic Australia book

New York
Battery Park
Ellis Island
Soho
Tribeca
Wall Street
Little Italy
Chinatown
Lower East Side
Brooklyn Bridge
BROOKLYN
EAST RIVER

RSEY
HUDSON RIVER
ONE WAY
BROADWAY
8ST
BROADWAY
Upper West Side
Times Square
Central Park
Rockefeller Center
33rd St
The Plaza
Upper East Side
East Village
Chrysler Building
Roosevelt Island
I ♥ NY
QUEENS

CHAPTER 1

Dear Diary

Why hello, old friend! It's been a little while since we've spoken, hasn't it? But guess what? Something very exciting is happening, Diary!

Would you like some *clues?*

It has something to do with APPLES.

It's *very big.*

And very noisy.

It never SLEEPS!

No, I'm not adopting a GIANT APPLE-EATING MONSTER. But now I come to think of it, that would be pretty cute!

I'm on my way to

New York!

You remember my parents are travel bloggers, which means they travel the world writing about different places. And this time, I get to go along!

Before we left, I had to take my puppy, Peachy Pie Sugar Snuggles, out to breakfast, so she would forgive me for being away for two whole weeks!

But she is staying with my Nanna and she *loves* Nanna.

I will check back in with you tomorrow, Diary, and tell you all about my first day in the Big Apple (that's New York's nickname, in case you were wondering!).

The Plaza

Dear Diary,

I am exhausted! One day in the Big Apple has really taken a bite out of me! But now I can see why they say New York is the city that never sleeps.

Even though I had literally the **BIGGEST DAY OF MY LIFE,** I do not want to sleep a wink! I just want to lie back, and remember it all happening again.

Let me tell you *all* about it.

Where to begin?

Let's start with Betsey, my big cousin, who met us at the airport.

When I say big, I don't mean BIG as in a giant. I mean, big, as in a grown-up! Cousin Betsey is so grown-up, she drives her very own *cab* (we call them taxis back home, but in New York it is *cab*). How cool is that?

Betsey wears a bright, fluffy pink coat. Her pink, glittery beanie has the *biggest* pompom in the world. And, I swear this is 100% true—Betsey has PINK HAIR!

Betsey drove us in her cab to the Plaza, which is the glitzy hotel where we are staying in New York city centre.

The chilly air kissed my cheeks when we got out of the cab. I could already tell winter in New York was going to be pretty *magical*.

I've never seen snow before, so when I saw piles of snow on the sidewalk, I may have gotten a bit overexcited.

Betsey held my hand, so I wouldn't slip on the pavement.

It was sweet of Betsey to look after me so well. But I accidentally (not so accidentally) slipped and fell into a snow pile.

Because, well, SNOW! Need I say more?

I hope I get to see snow falling before we have to leave New York. That would be *extra* magical.

I lay in a snowy, giggling heap. But Mum and Dad were keen to get inside the hotel.

The Plaza is over 100 years old, and has twenty storeys! I politely requested if we could switch from the 5th floor to the 20th floor at reception. The receptionist said yes! She said she liked my accent. Well, I liked hers!

Mum and Dad had to get ready for their first travel blog booking of the day. They are going to be blogging about New York buskers, and had lots of buskers to interview.

So they were letting Betsey take me on a New York adventure for the day. You know me, Diary—

I LOVE AN ADVENTURE!

After we checked out our room and put our luggage away, Betsey took me down to the lobby again, ready for our day in the Big Apple.

'But first, Paris, you gotta try the Plaza's desserts!' Betsey told me, leading me to the Palm Court.

Betsey didn't have to tell me twice—dessert for breakfast? Yes please!

Betsey was right. Dessert for breakfast was a VERY good idea. But as I was about to reach for a custard tart (*mmm, custard tart!*) Betsey told me to:

Betsey was right! Mmm, *blueberry bagel and cream cheese!*

'So, what's the best thing to do in New York?' I asked.

'Let's just say, you better get your skates on, Paris!' Betsey said.

Rockefeller Center

I would like to say that Betsey zoomed through the streets of New York. But when you are a cab driver in New York, you can't zoom, because there are so many cars! Mainly *cabs*, if I'm honest. Honking *cabs!*

'First stop, the Rockefeller Center,' said Betsey, pulling into a park.

I got out my *Visit New York* book, and thumbed through to find the Rockefeller Center.

I learnt that the Rockefeller Center was a complex of buildings, spanning *Fifth* and *Sixth Avenue*. (All the street names in New York City are numbers, like a grid.)

My book told me that these were '*art deco*' buildings, which made them sound pretty *fancy.* When Betsey and I made our way through the centre, I had to agree!

It wasn't just the buildings that were fancy. There was an epic Christmas tree towering over us, glowing with a million lights. It had to be the **BIGGEST CHRISTMAS TREE IN THE WORLD!**

And Betsey wasn't joking about needing skates.

There were kids and adults all skating around the rink—outside! I was particularly taken with an ice skater in a blue fluffy jacket and headphones. She was literally breakdancing on THE ICE!

When Betsey produced a pink pair of skates from her shoulder bag which were exactly Paris-sized, I couldn't wait a moment longer!

In my imagination, I looked as cool as the girl in the blue jacket. But in reality, I'd never skated before. Betsey held my hand. We shuffled around between everyone else.

At some point, I clung to the edge, while Betsey did some amazing *pirouettes* in the centre. If I could skate as well as that, I'd show off too!

After skating for an hour or so, we were pooped. So Betsey and I went to the bench to get our skates off. I found myself sitting next to a gorgeous Dalmatian called CAROLE, which I thought was a pretty cute name for a Dalmatian.

Diary, do you remember I am a dog whisperer? That means I can understand dog language!

Well, being a dog whisperer is pretty handy, because I found out heaps of cool things about Carole the Dalmatian. For example, she could actually skate really well, but wasn't allowed on the Rockefeller skate rink, because she is a dog.

'Are you talking to a dog?' asked someone on the other side of me. It was the cool girl with the fluffy blue jacket!

'Dogs speak my language!' I said proudly. 'Well, I speak theirs. Hey, you're a really good skater! My name is Paris, by the way. This is my first day in New York! And my first time on skates!'

'I'm Miley,' said the girl, in a thick New York accent. I liked Miley straightaway.

'Hey, Paris, do you reckon you can ask your dog-friend if she's seen my Broadway tickets? They're in my yellow spotty wallet.'

'Broadway! Isn't that where all the world-famous musicals happen?' I said.

Miley smiled. 'Sure is! Broadway is where the most famous musicals and plays in the world are performed, all day. And all night!'

MY HEART FLUTTERED.

Paris's Favourite Things

- My family
- My best friend, Jemima Wells

- DOGS
- Singing
- MUSICALS

- Dessert!

While I was busy feeling excited about musicals, I realised that Miley didn't look so excited.

'What is it, Miley?' I asked.

'My twin brother, Jed, and I see a Broadway show every year for our birthday. It's kind of tradition. This year, we were meant to see *Oodles of Poodles*—it's a new musical about POODLES! But, I, um . . . lost the tickets.'

Miley went quiet. I felt really bad for my new friend.

I asked Carole the Dalmatian, but Carole wagged her tail and barked twice to tell me dogs weren't allowed to see Broadway musicals, so she paid no attention to Broadway tickets.

But then I had a thought. Carole might not know where Miley's tickets and wallet were, but I'm actually a pretty good detective when it comes to finding lost stuff in AMAZING cities.

'I think I can help,' I told Miley. 'But first, I need to know where you were, when you last saw the tickets.'

'It was yesterday morning,' said Miley. 'Our moms had taken us up the Empire State building to check out the sunrise.

They know how much we both love the NYC skyline. They gave us the tickets there, which I put in my yellow spotty wallet. But when I went to check the show times this morning, I couldn't find my wallet! It must have fallen out of my bag.'

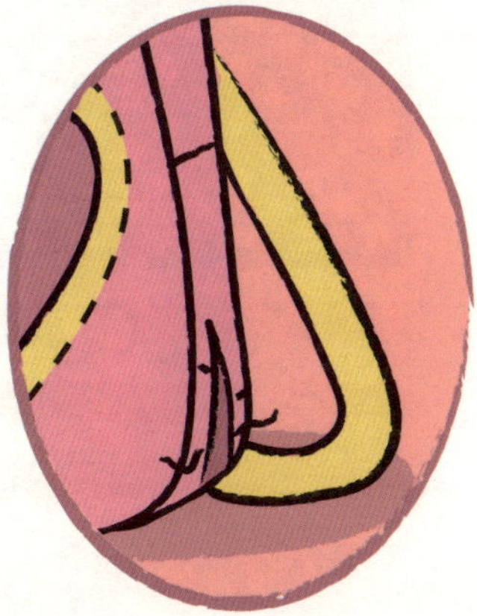

Miley showed me her pink backpack. Sure enough, there was a wallet-sized hole at the bottom, where some stitching had come undone.

'Hmm, yesterday morning,' I said. 'Empire State Building.'

'You ready to roll, Paris?' asked Betsey, hanging her skates over her shoulder.

'Any chance you could take us to the Empire State Building, Bets?' I asked.

CHAPTER 4

Empire State Building

The Empire State Building was close enough to walk to, but there wasn't a moment to waste. So Betsey cabbed us down *Fifth Avenue* to *33rd Street.*

The Empire State Building is pretty famous. So I already knew a little bit about it. For example, the Empire State Building is 102 storeys and more than 400 metres high! That's as if eight Olympic swimming pools stood on top of each other!

We jumped in one of the 73 lifts (73!) and made it to the top of the Empire State Building.

Miley, Betsey and I made our way around the top of the Empire State Building. The first time round, I looked super-duper hard on the ground for Miley's yellow spotted wallet.

The second time round, I saw something yellow and spotty through a sea of legs. I dove for the wallet.

'Hey!' yelled a kid. 'Watch it!'

The yellow wallet was just beyond my fingertips. I wiggled through the leggy sea, got my fingers trodden on, until at last . . .

'Gotcha!' I cried.

'A squirrel!' yelled Miley.

It took me a moment to realise I hadn't grabbed Miley's wallet. I'd grabbed someone's yellow spotted beanie! And I wasn't the only one. A grey squirrel was pulling the other end of the beanie, like we were playing tug-of-war.

'Hey! That's my beanie!' cried a girl.

I let go and apologised. But the squirrel was obsessed with the beanie. It grabbed it, leapt over all our heads, and disappeared in the crowd.

'Are you OK?' I asked the girl, who was rubbing her cold head.

'Hardly! A SQUIRREL just stole my beanie!' she said.

After we left the drama of the stolen beanie, we decided to take in the view. New York City looked like a toy town from the Empire State Building.

'Hey, we're on an island!' I said. 'I had no idea!'

'Yep,' said Miley. 'We call this island Manhattan. It's connected to mainland America by five bridges. Look, that's the Brooklyn Bridge! And if we go that way, we'll see the Statue of Liberty!'

'And that's Central Park, right?' I said, on our fourth round. Central Park was a long strip of nature in the middle of all the buildings.

'Sure is!' said Miley. 'We had pretzels for breakfast in Central Park yesterday.'

I brightened. 'You did? If your spotty wallet isn't on the Empire State Building, it might be in Central Park!'

Central Park

Betsey pulled up in front of the Metropolitan Museum of Art, and the

three of us ran through an avenue of leafless trees into Central Park. We made footprints in the snow.

'You should see Central Park in summer, Paris!' said Miley. 'Everything is so *green!*'

'My favourite season is autumn,' said Betsey. 'I can't get enough of those YELLOW leaves.'

'I'm liking Central Park in winter,' I said. 'I feel like I am inside a fairytale!'

Neigh!

I would have expected to see dogs in Central Park. But horses?

Neigh! Sure enough, two horses clopped towards us, pulling a fancy white carriage. I couldn't help but gasp. Now I was definitely inside a FAIRYTALE!

'We'll cover much more ground by carriage than on foot!' I said to Miley and Betsey. 'Hey, what are your names, horsies?'

'Ermine and Everdeen,' said the man, driving the carriage.

ZOO

There are not many places in the world which have:

- One zoo
- Three lakes
- Seven fountains
- 136 acres of woodland
- 9,000 benches

- 36 bridges and arches
- Athletic fields
- Sheep fields
- Children's play parks

- Squirrels
- Ducks
- Birds
- Turtles

- And an ice-skating rink!

As Ermine and Everdeen pulled us through Central Park, I sang songs I knew about New York. The whole time, my eyes were peeled, looking for Miley's lost wallet.

'As much as I LOVE snow, it's making it tricky to find your wallet, Miley,' I said. 'Where'd you say you had pretzels? Maybe your wallet dropped out there.'

'There!' said Miley, pointing. But she was pointing to a green pretzel cart parked under a leafless tree.

Ermine and Everdeen pulled to a halt and we piled out of the carriage.

'Pretzels for three please!' I said to the pretzel lady. She handed us each a GIANT knot of bread.

'You haven't seen a yellow spotty wallet, have you, Mam?' I asked the pretzel lady. She shook her head. I scoured the ground, pushing my boots through the snow. But there was no wallet.

'Excuse me! Excuse me!' I asked a passing poodle, who seemed to know her stuff. 'Any chance you've seen a yellow spotty wallet?'

The poodle's name was *Ella Fitzgerald*, named after a famous New York singer. She was definitely the right poodle to ask. She wagged her little tail, saying, 'I think I have!

Follow me!'

'Come, guys!' I said, running after her.

We sprinted through the snow and past a frozen lake.

'What's that?' I asked, pointing at an amazing angel statue rising out of the lake.

'That's the Angel of the Waters. The Bethesda Fountain,' said Miley.

She was majestic, with her snow covered wings! A REAL ANGEL!

Ella Fitzgerald kept running so we had to keep up!

Ella finally stopped, right near a carousel. Sure enough, there was something spotty and yellow buried in the snow ahead of us.

'Miley, look! Ella Fitzgerald found your wallet!' I yelled.

But when I dove for it, a squirrel appeared from nowhere, and beat me to it.

'It's not your wallet, Miley. It's someone's scarf!' I said. By then, the squirrel was bounding through the snow, with the yellow spotty scarf trailing behind like a flag.

We thanked Ella Fitzgerald and the three of us collapsed in the snow, exhausted. Miley showed me how to swipe my arms and legs like windscreen wipers. When we got up, I saw two angels in the snow!

But Miley's smile vanished. 'It's sad Jed and I won't be seeing *Oodles of Poodles*,' said Miley. 'It's meant to be really good.'

'Don't give up yet!' I said.

Just then, we heard some pretty strange sounds.

'Speaking of animals, are there bears in Central Park?' I said.

Miley laughed. 'Of course! There's a zoo right over there. We went there yesterday, for our birthday. Jed loves monkeys.'

My face lit up. Because after dogs, monkeys are literally my NEXT FAVOURITE animal.

Paris's Favourite Animals

1. Dogs

2. Monkeys

3. Polar bears

4. Sloths

5. Giraffes.

Then, I had a thought.

'Miley!' I cried. 'Don't you see? You dropped your wallet at the zoo! That's why we didn't find it in Central Park!'

Central Park Zoo

After spending a bit of time with the Gentoo penguins, the grizzly bears and the red panda, we finally made it to the snow monkey enclosure. As expected, the monkeys were monkeying about, throwing nuts at each other.

My heart beat faster, when I saw one of the monkeys was sitting on a yellow spotty rectangle.

'Look, Miley! Your wallet!' I said, pulling Miley's sleeve.

Now we'd finally found Miley's wallet (for **REAL** this time), we had one tiny problem. It was inside the monkey enclosure. And we were outside. In times like these, I wished I spoke *monkey!*

I thought I would give it a whirl anyway.

'Hey, monkey! Yes, you with the lovely face! Any chance my friend Miley can have her wallet back?'

The monkey poked out its tongue at me. Ahem! Rude.

I tried to think like a monkey. If I had just found myself a lovely spotty cushion for my bony bottom, would I give it up? Not easily.

Which made me think . . .

'Betsey, is there any chance you've had enough of your beanie?' I said.

Betsey patted her pink beanie protectively. 'It's kind of my favourite,' she said. 'But, since it's my favourite cousin asking . . . ' Betsey pulled off her beanie. I hugged her.

'Now to get the beanie to the monkey!'

I didn't even have time to come up with a plan before the beanie was snatched out of my hand by a cheeky monkey! It pulled it over its eyes and immediately fell off the branch!

I tried not to laugh.

But it looked so cute and funny.

Another monkey yanked Betsey's beanie free, and flew through the air to another branch. It had a beanie tug-of-war with yet another monkey, before a fourth monkey appeared from nowhere, snatched the beanie, and carried it over to the monkey sitting on Miley's wallet.

The wallet-sitting monkey looked so pleased with its prize, it jumped up, and the wallet tumbled off the branch, to the ground.

But that was when I realised something pretty DEPRESSING.

It wasn't Miley's yellow spotty wallet. It was actually a yellow spotty cushion, perhaps from a baby's pram.

'Sorry,' I said to both Miley and Betsey, because I still hadn't found Miley's wallet, and now I'd lost Betsey's super-cool beanie.

'It's nothing a *hotdog* won't fix,' said Betsey, folding me in a forgiving hug. 'What do you think?'

Miley and I nodded. I was getting pretty hungry after all our running around.

The Met

If anyone ever tells you that eating a steaming *hotdog*, covered in mustard, on the steps of The Met won't fix everything, they are wrong.

'Mmm, so good,' I mumbled, between bites.

The Met stands for The Metropolitan Museum of Art, and is the LARGEST museum in America. Betsey told me all about her favourite paintings in the art gallery.

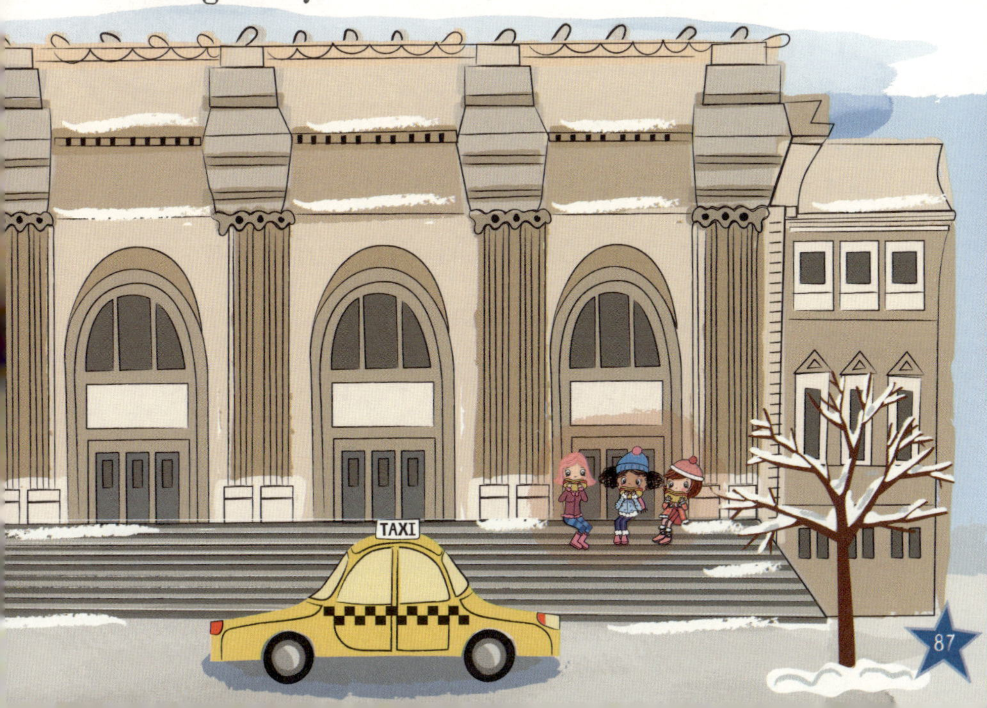

But Miley was quiet.

'Don't worry, Miley,' I said, taking her hand. 'We'll find your wallet.' But even I knew that New York City was so big, that finding a yellow spotty wallet was going to be tricky.

'It's a pity you didn't lose your wallet at the Statue of Liberty,' said Betsey, wiping her mustardy hands on a napkin. 'My friend Sam works for Lost and Found at the Statue of Liberty. He's always finding cool stuff, like people's

wedding rings, and mobile phones. Once, he found a garden gnome!'

Miley's face changed right then. And it wasn't just because the sun peeked through the grey sky. Or because Sam once found a garden gnome.

'We did go to Statue of Liberty yesterday!' said Miley. 'We took the ferry across to Ellis Island, so we could climb the statue's crown at sunset!'

Now I was beaming too.

'*All aboard!*' called Betsey, who was already opening her cab door.

Ellis Island

The ferry gate was closing, just as Betsey pulled into the taxi zone.

'Run!' I cried.

We sprinted, and just made it. The ferry was super crowded. It was hard to find a place to breathe, let alone squeeze through, so we could find Miley's spotty wallet. As we burst onto the ferry deck, I inhaled the chilly afternoon air.

'Here, take my scarf, Paris,' said Miley, wrapping her woollen scarf around me. 'You're shivering!'

Miley was such a sweet friend. I really hoped that Sam had Miley's spotty wallet at Lost and Found, so Miley and her brother would get to see *Oodles of Poodles* on Broadway.

While I gazed up at the Statue of Liberty's crown, I asked Betsey a question. 'Why is she called the Statue of Liberty anyway?'

'LIBERTY means freedom,' said Betsey. 'France gave the statue as a gift to the USA over 150 years ago. They wanted to celebrate freedom and democracy, and the friendship between the two countries.'

'The statue has welcomed immigrants arriving to New York by harbour for decades!' said Miley. 'Did you know that New York is one of the most multicultural cities on earth?'

'She does look very welcoming!' I said. 'But I was already feeling pretty welcome in the Big Apple, thanks to you two!'

When the ferry docked on Ellis Island, we raced straight up to see Sam.

'Nup. No spotty wallets here. Sorry!' said Sam. 'Unless you mean these?' He held up a pair of yellow spotty kids' socks.

'Um, who loses their socks at the Statue of Liberty?' I said.

From nowhere, a little grey squirrel appeared and whipped the yellow spotty socks from Sam's hands.

'Hey! They don't belong to you!' said Sam.

The squirrel darted off through the crowds.

Miley was looking pretty glum. I knew why too. We'd retraced Miley's steps from yesterday—up the Empire State Building, all around Central Park, to the Central Park Zoo and now to the Statue of Liberty. We'd found lots of yellow spotty things. But we hadn't found Miley's yellow spotty wallet.

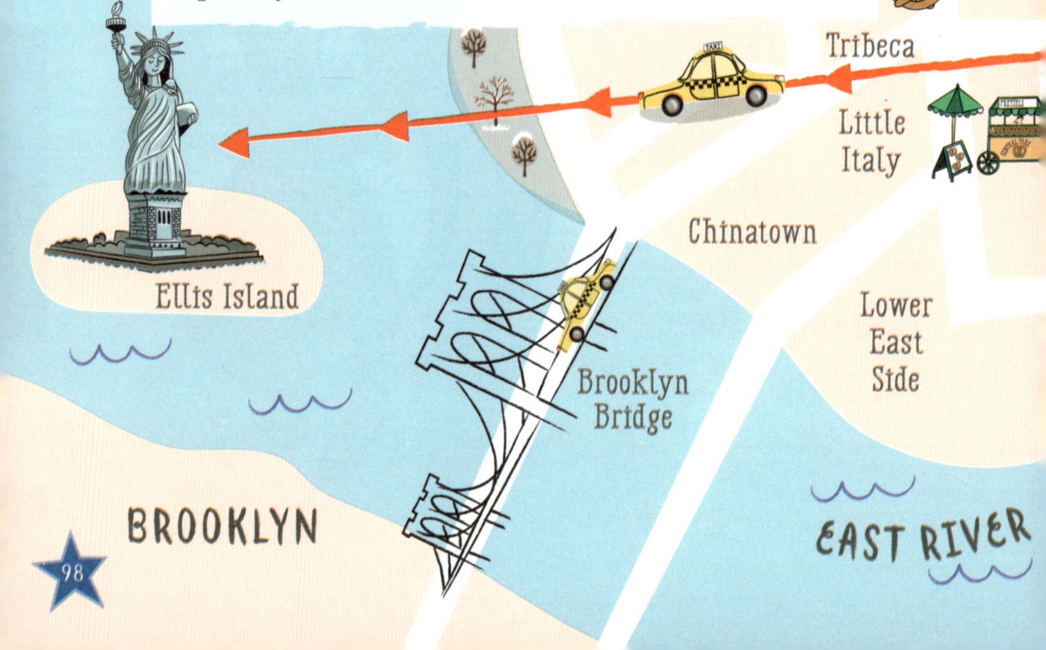

'Fancy a climb to the Statue of Liberty's crown?' I asked. 'I have something to show you, Miley.'

Statue of Liberty

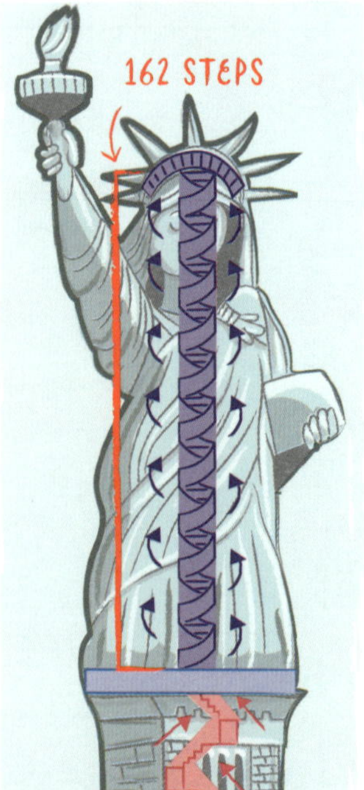

We climbed *162 steps*, **NARROW** steps from the statue's feet all the way to the crown. As we popped out the top, I gasped. New York City looked so spectacular, covered in a white, snowy blanket.

The pale sun was close to the horizon. If only I could see snow falling. It would be like being in a *snow globe!*

'What did you want to show me, Paris?' asked Miley.

'I figured if you can't go to Broadway, then Broadway should come to you,' I said.

I cleared my throat, and sang one of my favourite songs from one of my FAVOURITE musicals of all time—*Animal Talk*, which is all about a girl who can talk to animals. The other people on top of the statue's crown crowded around to listen.

Halfway through the song, the squirrel leapt out from nowhere, and landed in a man's fluffy hat. She looked like she was listening to me sing!

'That was so beautiful!' said Miley, when I finished. 'Even that squirrel loved it! Look!'

Just as she pointed though, the squirrel hat-hopped through the crowd, grabbed a very spotty banana from a toddler's hands, and disappeared around the other side of the crown.

'That squirrel really **LOVES** yellow spotty things, doesn't she?' I said.

Just then, a yellow spotty idea started taking shape in my mind. I realised I knew where Miley's wallet was! And this time I was as sure as *mustard* on a *hotdog*.

'Come, Miley! Betsey! We have to find that squirrel!'

We ran around and around the crown. But we couldn't find the squirrel anywhere.

'If you were a squirrel, where would you hide to stay warm in a New York winter?' I asked the others.

I spotted the squirrel perched on the Statue of Liberty's nose. She disappeared inside the crown.

We ran to the nose and peered down.

The inside of the statue was black, black, black. Slowly, my eyes adjusted and I saw two beady eyes glowing back at me, and . . .

lots of yellow spotty things!

Spotty scarves.

Spotty beanies.

Spotty socks.

A spotty apron.

A spotty jumper.

Spotty knickers!

'Look!' I said. 'There are more squirrels. *Baby* squirrels!'

'The mama squirrel must have been collecting yellow spotty things to make a yellow spotty nest for her babies,' I said.

'Because there are no leaves on the trees,' said Miley.

'Because it's *winter!*' said Betsey.

We couldn't take our eyes off those adorable baby squirrels in their yellow spotty nest.

'Do you think my wallet is in there?' whispered Miley.

I hummed softly (because the mama squirrel likes music), reached inside, and felt around for something small and rectangular. Careful not to upset the squirrel babies, I drew out Miley's yellow spotty wallet.

Miley hugged the wallet to her chest. Then she removed the Broadway tickets and handed the wallet back to me.

'But Miley, we've searched the whole of New York City for your wallet!' I said.

'The squirrels need it more than me,' said Miley. 'Besides, I have my tickets!'

Carefully, I returned the wallet to the yellow spotty nest, inside the Statue of Liberty.

'Goodbye, little friends,' I whispered, before taking 162 stairs down to the statue's feet.

★★★

Miley used Betsey's mobile to let her mums know she'd found the tickets, just in time for the show. She told them she'd meet Jed in the theatre foyer.

As she was talking, her face fell.

'What is it?' I asked Miley, when she was off the phone.

'Jed's not feeling well,' said Miley. 'He's not going to get to see *Oodles of Poodles* after all.' But as she spoke, her face changed. Suddenly, she was smiling at me. It was like she'd just found her yellow spotty wallet all over again!

'You know what this means, Paris?' she asked.

'I do?' I thought I did. But I kept my fingers crossed in my pockets, just in case. Was Miley going to say what I *hoped* she was going to say?

'You can come to the Broadway show with me instead!' said Miley. 'We can see *Oodles of Poodles* together!'

We had the **BIGGEST** hug of the day. Betsey, though, was tapping her foot.

'You kids better jump in the cab, if you're going to make the show in time!' said Betsey. 'Paris, I'll call your parents and let them know.'

Times Square was lit up like a Rockefeller Christmas tree. There were thousands of colours and lights and moving screens, shining in every direction. I couldn't get too distracted, though. We had a Broadway show to get to!

Broadway

The *Oodles of Poodles* musical was incredible!

1
2

When it was finished, I met Betsey outside the theatre, ready to take me back to my hotel.

But I felt a sad feeling in my tummy. I knew it was time to say goodbye to my new friend, Miley.

'Promise you'll visit again?' asked Miley.

'Are you kidding? I'll be back in a HEARTBEAT!' I said. We exchanged postal addresses and hugs. I couldn't stop the tear running down my cheek.

But I felt something else too.

'Look, Paris. Snow!' whispered Miley.

Sure enough, tiny flakes fell on our noses and eyelashes. I stuck out my tongue to taste it. It was cool and fresh. The snow was so light!

'Magical!' I said, giving Miley one last hug, before jumping into Betsey's cab.

I ♥ NY
I ♥ NY
NOVOTEL
BSHC
TONH
TAXI

Hey Paris!

It was so so fun, hanging out with you in NYC! Have you booked another trip soon? I hope so!
Hey, thanks for helping me find my Broadway tickets! I was so happy we could see the show together. And guess what? Jed and I have been collecting yellow spotty things for the squirrel family! Mom takes us up the Statue of Liberty every Saturday, for our special spotty delivery. Cute, hey!

'Til next time you're in the Big Apple.
Your pal - Miley

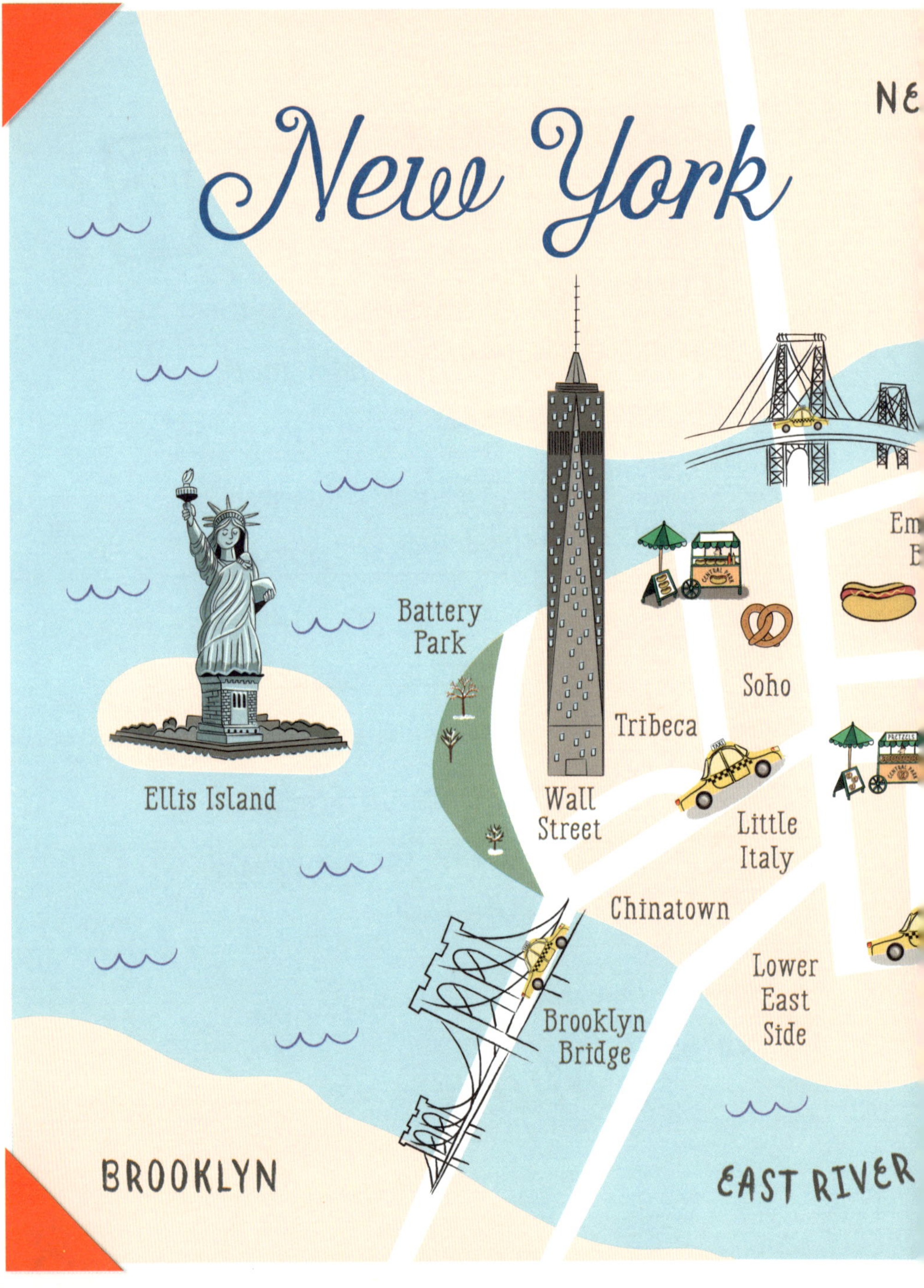
New York
Battery Park
Ellis Island
Soho
Tribeca
Wall Street
Little Italy
Chinatown
Lower East Side
Brooklyn Bridge
BROOKLYN
EAST RIVER
CENTRAL PARK
PRETZELS
TAXI

RSEY
HUDSON RIVER
ONE WAY
BROADWAY
8 ST
BROADWAY
Upper West Side
Times Square
Central Park
Rockefeller Centre
33rd St
The Plaza
Upper East Side
East Village
Chrysler Building
Roosevelt Island
I ♥ NY
QUEENS

NEW YORK
I ♥ NY
International Airport